E
EVERYDAY
WITCH

cute gaver girl
is cool

EVIE EVERYDAY WITCH

SECRET MAGIC

Elena Paige

Text and artwork copyright 2019 © Elena Paige

The right of Elena Paige to be identified as the author of this work has been asserted by her.

Illustrations by Stephanie Parcus

Cover design by Deranged Doctor Design

Published by Angelos Publishing

Paperback ISBN: 978-1-925557-74-9
Hardback ISBN: 978-1-925557-75-6
E-book ISBN: 978-1-925557-73-2
Audio Book ISBN: 978-1-925557-76-3

 A catalogue record for this book is available from the National Library of Australia

*Dedicated to **you** for having the courage to be YOURSELF!*

Chapter 1

Have you ever met a witch before?

No? You have now. Hi. I'm Evie. Evie Everyday. My mom calls me her everyday witch. My dad calls me his little rebel witch because I never practice magic like I'm supposed to. I read instead. Both my parents are witches too.

All I've ever wanted is to be a regular girl and go to a regular school. In the books I read, normal kids are friendly and kind, and learn fun stuff like maths, English and geography. Instead I go to a school for witches, called Pergoria. We learn boring stuff, like how to make potions, how to fly on broomsticks, how to disappear and reappear in different places. You know? Everyday witch stuff. Nothing special. Or useful. And the kids there are plain old mean.

We just moved into a new town called Wyndemere. No witches here. It's full of normal people. How exciting is that? We used to live in Fancy Hollow with other witches, but dad had enough of our neighbor Mr Garbunkle. He would practice calamity magic all night long and keep dad awake. In case you're wondering, calamity magic is where you make furniture come to life. If you ever get the chance - trust me, don't try it!

Furniture gets really rowdy and noisy when it has a personality. Anyways, Mr Garbunkle spread rumors that dad attacked his couch and broke his dining chairs. Which totally isn't true. So dad decided we needed a fresh start.

The first thing I did when we moved here was find the local school, Wyndemere Elementary.

Every night when Mom and Dad would tuck me into bed, I would ask, "Can I go to Wyndemere? Please?" And every night they would say no. They made me fly all the way to Pergoria every day. But this past Halloween, when I asked if I could dress up in an orange school building costume, my parents finally got the hint.

The next day, Mom said I could go to Wyndemere in the new school year. Yes, she did! Dad grumbled about it. But Mom's the boss in our family.

Me, Evie Everyday, finally gets to be an everyday kid!

Today is my first day in sixth grade, and my knees are shaking like I'm about to be attacked by a giant bulldog.

Did I mention dogs don't like witches? It's true. One time, Mrs. Parker, the town snoop, walked her dog all the way to the top of the hill where we live. No one comes up this way. Normal people are too scared. But not Mrs. Parker. I bet she'd sell one of her own children for fresh gossip.

Our house looks like an old haunted shack from the outside, and people keep away. Anyways, her dumb dog ran through our house, scared my cat Mr. Nipkins half to death, and knocked over my mom's new potion set. She wasn't happy. Nope. Not one bit.

Luckily, Mrs. Parker could only see what we wanted her to: an old empty shack that came to life, moving and shaking and talking. It frightened the bejeebers out of her. I still laugh thinking about how fast she bolted down the hill with her ditzy dog. I sent some whizzing firecrackers after them for good measure. At that speed I reckon they could have both launched to the moon. Anyhow, Mrs. Parker hasn't come back since. Neither has her dog.

As I walk up the giant steps of Wyndemere, I elbow my backpack. Sylvie is making *scritch-scratch* noises from inside. She's my pet bat. Oh, don't worry, I haven't got a real live bat in my bag. Bats aren't allowed in school, silly. At least, I don't think they are.

I turned Sylvie into a pair of glasses. She's awesome to look out of. When I put her on, I can see things about people. Like what their favorite food is, and whether they own a cat or not. You know, useful information.

"Stop right there," comes a voice from behind me.

I turn around slowly, scared to see who that big bossy voice belongs to. Just my luck. It's a teacher.

"Are you new?" she asks. She's tall and skinny and dressed in a tight, black gym suit. She looks like a balloon that's about to pop. Her hair is tied into a bun so tight her eyes look like tiny ninja slits.

"Yes, I am. A new normal kid. At this normal school. Brand new. That's me." I hate the way I stutter when I'm nervous and say stupid stuff.

She looks me over, suspicion squinting from both her eyes. She scrunches her nose at me.

"Name?" she commands.

"Evie. Evie Everyday. Nice to meet you." I reach my hand out for hers. Mom told me it's polite to shake hands with Lamrons. That's what I call normal people. It's the word normal spelled backward, get it? I made it up myself.

Drool drips from the teacher's mouth onto my honey-colored braids. She's twice my height

and hunched over me now, the way I imagine Maleficent in *Sleeping Beauty* when she turns into a dragon. Talk about terrifying.

She eyes my clothes. "It's important to fit in at this school. We don't like troublemakers." She snorts at me like I imagine a pig would. I don't know for sure as I've never met a pig.

I have a feeling this is her way of being extra polite because I'm new. She lunges away in her tight exercise gear. I'm guessing she's the gym teacher. I had been looking forward to gym. But now, not so much.

I let go of all self-control and my knees start shaking again. Other students are starting to arrive. Why are they all wearing black? I should have done my research.

They look pretty boring in black, but that doesn't change the fact that I look like a clown at a funeral. I reach for my bag and wonder if there's time to change my outfit without anyone noticing. I'm trying really hard not to use magic, and someone might see me. I decide against it, and drop my bag on the ground, anger getting the better of me.

"Ouch!" says a voice from my bag.

Don't worry, that's not Sylvie. Bats don't talk! Now that would be weird. That's Mr. Nipkins. I call him Nip for short. And in case you're wondering, I didn't bring my cat to school either. Well, not exactly. I turned him into a diary first.

"Sorry, Nip!" I call back. I didn't mean to hurt him.

"Who's Nip?" The voice is bright and cheery and coming from behind me.

"Hi," I say, looking this girl up and down. She's not wearing black. I'm confused.

"Hi. I'm Isabel. But you can call me Izzy for short. You're new."

"Yep. New and normal."

She looks at me with a big smile. "Nice clothes. Super original. Where did you get the orange-and-pink striped stockings from? I'd love a pair. The local shops only sell black clothes around here so I have to make my own." Izzy curls her top lip and scrunches her nose at the kids, all dressed in black, walking past her.

"I can bring you a pair. I have lots. But I think you should try harder to be normal. It's important to fit in."

Did I mention I have never fitted in? At my old school, Pergoria, I was always considered weird.

Izzy's silky yellow dress flutters in the wind and she shakes her long red hair out. "Normal? Who wants to be boring old normal? That's the problem with this town. Everyone is super normal. I'd rather be new and original. I'd rather be myself."

I wonder what she means? Why isn't she happy with nice, normal people? Why doesn't she want to fit in? I'm confused by her. Fitting in is all I've ever wanted.

"Normal is awesome!" I yell awkwardly. I'm definitely going to wear black tomorrow. And since I made a pact not to use my wand, even at home, I'm already planning on using the black curtains in my dad's office. He won't notice. He's always so busy drafting new laws for witches.

Izzy laughs. I'm not sure why.

"So who is Nip?" she asks.

"Nip? No one special. It's just the nickname I gave my diary."

"Super. Can I see it?"

"Sure." I pull Nip from my bag and lean my head down to him so no one else hears me. "Don't say a word. Be normal, got it? You promised." I give him a giant you'll-be-in-big-trouble-if-you-break-your-promise kind of look and smile at Izzy.

She laughs again. What's with that?

"Super cool looking diary! I've never seen anything so cute. Not ever!" She strokes the purple fur cover as if it's a cat. Well, it is, but she doesn't know that. I pull it away from her in case Nip starts purring.

"Sorry! I don't know why I did that. Anyway, we'd better get to class. I'm in sixth grade. You?"

"Me too," I say.

I'm not sure it's a good idea to be spotted with someone so weird on my first day. I look around for someone to tag along after. Someone dressed in black.

I pick up my backpack, and Izzy looks at me funny. Then she looks at my bag. Her smile becomes twice its size. I shove Nip back into my bag and wonder what she's smiling at.

Oh no! Freshly popped corn is popping itself out of my bag and all over the school steps. Students are catching handfuls and cheering me on. My face feels hotter than the hot corn. Pops must have snuck into my bag. How could he?

Pops is my pet corncob. Well, he's kind of my pet. He was just an ordinary corncob once. I used a potion on him and brought him to life. He doesn't talk. But he does have these cute little green spindly legs and tiny brown kernels for eyes. And he's very emotional. He's been popping corn like crazy for over a week every time I mention I'm going to school without him.

I shove my hand into my bag and grasp that crazy corncob. I squeeze him tight. He likes that. It calms him down.

"You're definitely not normal, are you?" says Izzy, stuffing her face with popcorn. "I like it."

"I am. I am normal!" I yell as if my life

depends on it.

Luckily, Pops settles down, the popcorn stops spilling from my bag, and the kids all move away. Phew! I got this.

"Miss Everyday. My office. Now!"

It's that gym teacher from earlier. She's as red as a bobbing apple at Halloween.

"I'm going to follow that teacher like a normal kid." I'm glad at least to get away from Izzy. She asks too many questions.

She laughs again. "You're too cool. You get to go to Principal Rogers' office on your first day. That's definitely not normal. I'll save you a seat in class."

No, I want to yell, but instead I'm wondering what she means. Is the gym teacher the principal? I guess I'll find out.

Chapter 2

I skip down the hall after Mrs. Rogers. That's
when I notice none of the other kids are skipping.
They're gliding. I try to copy, though not very
well. I feel like a cat dizzy from too much
dancing. Cats aren't very good dancers, let me
tell you.

My shoes make this squeaking, screeching
noise. I figure it must be the gold glitter all over
them. What? So I love glitter. Except right now,
glitter doesn't seem so popular at this school.
I stomp my foot. Why didn't I do my research?
This day was going to be perfect. And so far, it's

totally ruined.

I suck back my tears. I'm more determined than ever to fit in. I can do this!

I enter Mrs. Rogers's office. It's black. Black chair, black desk, black walls, and black death stare. She's not happy.

"What is the meaning of this?" She waves her hand at me and then grabs my backpack from my shoulder. Spit froths from her lips again, but this time I step back just in time to miss the tsunami.

"Sit!"

For once, I haven't got any words.

She empties my backpack onto her desk. It's all there. My life revealed for her to see. How did my wand and flute get in my bag? I huff out my madness. It was either Nip or Pops.

Mrs. Rogers picks up my white wooden wand. She doesn't say a word, her face is impossible for me to read. I can't tell what she's thinking. I bet my mom would love Mrs. Rogers on her team at the annual Witches Poker Tournament.

Mrs. Rogers picks up Pops.

I half close my eyes and wait for him to start popping again. But he doesn't. Next, she flicks through Nip. And finally, she picks up Sylvie.

Setting them all down again, she opens my lunchbox. Her forehead becomes as wrinkled as an elephant's behind. She's not happy. Not one bit.

She picks out the fairy bread in disgust and throws it in the bin. How can anyone throw away soft bread smothered in butter and covered in rainbow sprinkles without so much as a nibble? She's one tough teacher. She closes the lunchbox, drops the elephant face for an I-love-you kinda face, and sits down across the desk. I'm more confused than ever.

She clears her throat. "You're a *lovely* girl. A *ray* of sunshine. But I can tell there's more to you, am I right?"

Her tone reminds me of my Auntie Floss just

before she's about to serve you a burned dinner. She's good at convincing you that you weren't very hungry in the first place.

I nod my head. Not sure why, but it's all I can think to do.

"I can tell you want to fit in at this school. Right?" Her face is positively gleaming. Maleficent has turned into Tinkerbell right before my eyes.

I nod my head again. Seriously! What is wrong with me? Why am I nodding as if I have no control over my body?

"I can make that happen. I can make sure that *everyone* at Wyndemere thinks you're wonderful. You'd like that, wouldn't you, Evie?"

I nod my head again. I'm a lost cause.

"You'll be the toast of the town. The most popular girl in school. The most *normal* girl here."

She uses the word. My word. *Normal.*

Mrs. Rogers has gone from feared teacher to my superhero in five seconds. She's like the sprinkles on my bread. The bell on my witch's hat. The magic in my spell. She has me. And she knows it.

Mrs. Rogers opens up a desk draw and pulls out a black dress. It's just my size. I can tell.

"Would you like to wear this?" She beams a smile at me, her polished white teeth catching a ray of sunshine and spritzing light around the room, just like Cinderella's do in my imagination.

I nod and smile so much my cheeks start hurting. She's helping me be normal. Not *just* normal. She's helping me be *cool* normal. Like everyday-best-most-popular-kid-in-school normal. Who needs research? I have Mrs. Rogers on my side.

"Go on, try it on." She hands me the dress and turns her back.

I chuck off my sneakers, pull off my striped stockings, rip off my green top, and waddle out of my purple skirt. I feel the cold calm of the black dress as I glide it on. I feel awesome. Yes, I do. Yes, yes, yes. Black is awesome. Black is cool!

"I'm ready," I say, speaking for the first time since arriving in her office.

Mrs. Rogers turns around slowly. She looks all elephant Maleficent again, but only for a few seconds. She's soon back to her Tinkerbell-Cinderella self.

I don't care. What does it matter anyway? All that matters is that she's on my side.

She picks up my old clothes and puts them in my backpack. She carefully places my wand, flute, Pops, Nip, and Sylvie back in there too. And my rainbow-colored lunch box. "You won't be needing these anymore. I'll hold on to them."

I burp suddenly. I don't know why. It just kind of forces itself out of my mouth. I need my friends with me, don't I?

Mrs. Rogers must be a mind reader. "You'll make new friends. Normal friends."

"Sure. Okay," I say.

Hey, before you go judging me, I want this normal thing more than you can imagine.

I finally want to fit in somewhere. To belong.

I was a total misfit at my old school. Pergoria is all about rules, tradition, and being the best. No new spells allowed. Only tried and tested magic permitted. And instead of making friends with other witches, you compete to be better than them. There's no way I'm going back, so it's important I fit in here. Super important!

"Before you go," Mrs. Rogers says with a voice so sweet it makes my fairy bread seem sour. She hands me a black pair of sneakers. Just my size too. "Your new friend Izzy. She's not like everyone else here at Wyndemere. She's different. You don't want to be different like her, do you?"

"No," I say. In my head I'm chanting, *Nope. Nada. No way!*

"Good. Stay away from her."

"Sure." This is fine by me. Everything is suddenly going my way. This terrible day has just turned into the best first day ever!

Chapter 3

I skip into class. Oops. I forgot—no skipping!

I change to gliding. I'm taking long, slow steps,

while drooping my shoulders like a monkey.

I need more practice at this gliding thing.

Just to be sure I'm not standing out, I pull out

my braids and shake my long hair out. Cool and

normal. That's me. I freeze in place. Everyone is

staring at me. And not in a good way.

"Welcome, Evie. We've been waiting for you."

The teacher looks nice. He's not much taller than

me and has the brightest yellow hair I've ever

seen. Not quite as bright as I imagine Prince

Charming would have, but close. He's writing on the chalkboard.

Everyone's still staring at me. I drop my face another inch to look like them. Then I notice Izzy. She's in the front row, so I'm not sure how I didn't see her until now. She's waving at me like crazy and pointing to the empty seat next to her. I scan the room as fast as my eyes can move for another chair, but they're all taken.

"Take a seat. Next to Izzy is fine, thank you. We're going to spend some time this morning doing introductions. Don't worry about being new. Everyone is technically new all over again on the first school day. Aren't you, kids?"

"Muh!" the class replies as one. They sound like a bunch of sheep. Dazed-out sheep.

"Yes, sir!" shouts Izzy.

What is with her? Why isn't she like the rest?

She leans over to me and whispers, "Where did your pretty clothes go?"

I shrug, frown, grimace, and look back at the

chalkboard. I bite my lip. My name's the first on the board. Oh no.

"Evie, since you're new, you can be the first bee on the honeycomb this morning. Step on up and tell us about yourself."

Metal springs go off in my head, sending crazy electrical messages to all the wrong places in my brain. I feel cursed, crazy, confused.

I stand up slowly and turn around. No words are coming. I'm not sure how to speak like a normal kid. I've only met Izzy so far, and I don't want to sound like her.

"Go ahead. Don't be shy. Tell us where you live, what school you've come from, and some hobbies you're into," says the teacher.

I feel my heart beat at least thirty more times. Still no words come out of my mouth.

The teacher chuckles. "All right, I'll go first, then. I'm Mr. Sanders. I have lived here in Wyndemere all my life. I've been a teacher for a year. I love watching ice-hockey games. My favorite food is Nutella pizza, and my favorite subject is math. See, it's not so hard. Your turn."

I glance over my shoulder at him. He does make me feel calm. I start off slowly. "My name is Evie. I'm just normal, that's all. I love wearing black. It's my favorite color," I lie.

The boy in the back row starts laughing. Not the kind of haha-that's-funny sort of laugh. More the haha-I'm-laughing-at-you kind of laugh.

Mr. Sanders clears his throat. "That's enough, Todd. Go on, Evie. Black is a very popular color at this school. In fact, it's the only color in the whole town."

"So I fit right in then!" I don't mean to sound so bubbly. I tone myself right down and start speaking like an mp3 with a glitch. "I live on the hill, just beyond the cemetery."

The kids all sit up as straight as a broomstick. It's like static electricity buzzed through the room and flew into everyone's brains at once. All eyes are on me. Big, round, curious eyes. They look like they just woke up from a deep trance. They all start whispering. Izzy is still smiling straight at me.

"Quiet, class. Settle down! This is very unlike

you," says Mr. Sanders.

But no one does. Instead they start yelling out questions at me.

"Are you a ghost?" squeals one boy. His face is covered in freckles.

"Are you a vampire?" says the girl next to Izzy. She stands up, puts one hand on her hip, and points her finger at me with her other hand.

I gulp. Did I say something wrong?

"She's a zombie!" yells a round kid as he throws gum at me. Bull's-eye. It lands right on my head and sinks into my hair.

"Maybe she's a witch," says Izzy. The room goes silent.

I gulp even harder. Where is Mrs. Rogers? She promised me I'd fit in and be liked.

"That's quite enough, class. Enough!" says Mr. Sanders. "That's no way to treat our new student. You can sit down please, Evie."

He waves his piece of chalk at the class, and they all slink back into their chairs. He leans in real close to me and whispers, "So are you a witch?"

"No! No, I'm not a witch!" I shoot Izzy the meanest stare I can muster. How did she know to say that? She smiles back at me. She's loopy, I decide. Mrs. Rogers is right. I need to stay away from her.

I stand up, mad as a monster, pick up the pen and book that's on the desk, and move to the back of the room. I kick the round kid that said I was a zombie in the leg and say, "Move or I'll turn you into a zombie too."

Luckily, he believes me and moves next to Izzy.

The class settles back down to dazed-out sheep, and take their turn standing up and introducing themselves. But I'm not listening.

All I can hear in my head going up and down, round and round, side to side, are the words "Are you a witch?"

I have to do something drastic. I have to take this to another level. I need to convince these kids I'm normal. Right here and now, I decide, I'm going to throw a party at my house. That will fix everything. And Izzy won't be invited.

Chapter 4

I'm messing with my hair in the mirror, getting ready for my second day of normal school. I finally got that gum out of my hair with my spare wand. My black wand. And I had to break my oath not to use magic.

All witches have two wands—a black one and a white one. Why two? The white one does white magic and the black one does black magic. We're not really meant to use the black one unless it's on an enemy. Yep, witches have enemies. You know, like demons, zombies, harpies, werewolves. And lizard men. The usual not-nice monsters.

I'm missing Sylvie and Nip, a lot. I'm even missing Pops a little. I refuse to listen to the gnawing in my stomach that says I shouldn't have left them with Mrs. Rogers. I'm sure they'll understand.

The rest of my first day at school was pretty good. Sandy, Gertrude, and Monique let me have lunch with them. They talked nonstop about some show they watch on TV. I wouldn't know, since I don't have a TV. But I think I did pretty well at lying.

I grab my spare bag and turn it black. I shove my party flyers into it. I stomp past the kitchen and tell Mom no more fairy bread for me. Luckily she's too busy as always to ask why. I head out the door. As I walk down the hill, I plan how I'm going to hand out all the party flyers. I haven't told Mom or Dad that we're hosting a party yet.

Or that I'm going to have to redecorate our rad rainbow house to basic black.

"Hey, Evie!"

I know that voice. It's Izzy. What's she doing up here? No one comes here. Without looking back, I run. I run like my house is a volcano, and it's erupted, and I'm about to get fried.

I stop at the bottom of the hill and catch my breath. I'm a fast runner, so I'm sure I've lost her.

"I love running in the morning too," says Izzy from right beside me. I consider changing myself into a snake and slinking away, but I left my spare wand at home. And I'm trying really hard not to use magic. Remember?

I roll my eyes at her, hoping she'll get the message. She doesn't. She just smiles, same as always.

"I brought breakfast for us to share." She reaches out her hand.

Is that what I think it is? The smell wafts up my nose and tickles my taste buds. I know that smell. It's freshly baked pineapple waffles with strawberry cream! A favorite witch's delight.

"I made them myself fresh this morning." Izzy bites into hers and makes *mmm* sounds. "So good."

I take it from her hand, too tempted to resist. I bite into the fluffy, crunchy, sweet, savory delight. It's deliciously divine. It tastes better than the ones my Grandma Iris makes. How does this regular girl know how to make pineapple waffles?

"Are you a witch?" I say.

"That would be super cool, but no. You are," she says back. Still smiling.

"I am not!"

"Yes, you are!"

"No, I'm not!"

"Yes, you are!"

We do this the whole way to school, while skipping and eating waffles together. Hey, cut me a break. I'm still learning this "be normal" stuff.

"I can't be your friend," I say as we get to the school wall. Monique is waving me over.

"I won't tell your secret, I promise. I'm sorry for blurting it out yesterday."

"It doesn't matter since I'm not a witch anyway. It's really important I fit in. You know, hang out with the right crowd."

Izzy half drops her smile. "I get it." She perks back up again. "And you are a witch." She is one persistent weed. And today she's dressed in bright pink! Bright pink! Can you believe that? It's my favorite color, and I'm dying to yell that I want a dress just like it. But I remind myself I'm very lucky to be wearing black.

"See ya, Izzy."

"Bye, Evie Everyday Witch!"

Humph! Would she stop already? Why is she convinced I'm a witch? I mean, I am. But how does she know?

Monique walks up and gives Izzy a death stare. Izzy smiles at her and skips through the school doors.

"Hey," I say. "I had the best day ever with you and Gertrude and Sandy yesterday. Want to come to a party at my place?"

"A party at your place? At the top of the hill? Will there be zombies?"

"No. I promise not to invite them. Only regular people are allowed to come."

Monique shudders. "Listen, I had a chat with the others, and I think you're a bit too weird for us." She flicks her hair and puts her hands on her hip, funky black jeans.

Before I can beg Monique to change her mind, Mrs. Rogers bursts out of the school doors. She smiles sweetly at me and then whacks Monique on the back, the way you hit someone when they're choking on a giant piece of candy. Monique slouches. Her face droops. "Hi, Mrs. Rogers. I was just telling Evie how normal she is and how much we love her." Her tone is flat and lifeless.

Huh?

Mrs. Rogers walks back through the front doors and disappears. I was going to ask her if I could have my stuff back, but she left too quickly. I turn back to Monique instead. "I thought you said you don't want to be my friend."

"I was just testing you. You know, to see if you fit in. And hey, you're the best. You can definitely hang out with us. When's your party?"

I believe her. I have to. I hand her a flyer from my bag. "Can you help pass some out?"

"Sure. Give them all to me, and I'll make sure everyone in the school gets one."

"Awesome," I say, forgetting to sound dull. I lower my head and the pitch of my

voice to sound like hers. "That would be
supercalifragilisticexpialidocious."

Oops. That word totally slipped out. Luckily,
Monique doesn't seem to care. She glides up
the stairs and through the front doors. I follow
behind. My glide is definitely improving. I'm really
getting a handle on this being normal thing.

As we get to class, Mr. Sanders announces that we need to vote for this year's school president. Sandy shoots her hand up.

"Yes, Sandy?" says Mr. Sanders. "Would you like to run for school president?"

"No, sir. I think Evie should be the school president."

My lips feel like they turn inside out to match my stomach. I think I'm excited, even though I don't even know what school president is.

"What do you think, Evie? Would you like to run for school president?"

Before I can answer, all the other students start chanting my name. My feet start dancing to the beat of "Evie, Evie, Evie."

"Hush, everyone. Let Evie speak," says Mr. Sanders.

"Sure. What do I have to do?" I can feel my face turning warmer and warmer.

"Well, you need to put together a list of all the things you'll do to make the school a better place. How you plan to help the students. Do you have any suggestions?"

Suggestions on how to make Wyndemere better? Um . . . My brain scans through everything I've experienced in my one day here. I want to say, "Bring some color into the place. Get rid of stew for lunch and replace it with fairy bread and pizza! And make the classes more interesting."

Don't get me wrong. Mr. Sanders is great and all, but a school with no gym, art, or drama class? Seriously, what's with that? Instead, I open my mouth and say, "I would make it compulsory to wear black. I would demand cauliflower soup be added to the lunch menu, and I would ask Mrs. Rogers if we can all stay after class and clean the school every day."

If Nip was here, he'd have bitten me for saying all that. He hates cleaning! And he hates cauliflower. So do I come to think of it. Why did I say that?

No one talks. They're hardly breathing. Mr. Sanders looks like a bat who's drunk too much Gillow Punch. That's punch made from sour apples and crushed avocados. He's greener than that!

For the first time ever, I notice Izzy isn't smiling. She's blinking so fast, I wonder if her eyes might fly right off her face. Just when I'm about to apologize, Todd, the boy who laughed at me yesterday, starts clapping like crazy. Yep! He does.

And then so does everyone else. As if that's not enough, they all start cheering. Mr. Sanders turns even more green than before. A tingling sensation sweeps up the back of my neck and across my face. I want to feel happy, but I'm torn. I lied again. And it worked. So I do what any eleven-year-old who's just lied to be popular would do—I bow. And they clap louder.

Mrs. Rogers storms through the door. Her spandex gym suit looks like it's about to burst at the seams. She's breathing so hard I can see hair dancing in and out of her nostrils. "What is the meaning of all this noise?"

The room goes deafeningly quiet. My hands are clammy, and my bottom lip trembles. I only dare move my eyeballs to see what Mr. Sanders is doing. He's more yellow than green now. He looks like he's so scared of Mrs. Rogers he might just pee his pants. My knees join in the shaking.

"Well? Explain!" says Mrs. Rogers.

"I—we—I mean, Evie—" Beads of sweat squirm their way down Mr. Sanders' forehead as he speaks. Is he scared of her? Are they all scared of her? Something isn't right. Why is everyone so fearful of Mrs. Rogers?

"It's my fault," I say, stepping toward her. "And I want my bag back." I fight back my tears. I don't want the class to get in trouble because of me.

Mrs. Rogers takes a few giant rhinoceros steps toward me. I swear the two hairy warts on either side of her mouth are moving up and down like they're about to jump off her face, turn into giant cockroaches with blaster guns, and shoot me all the way out of this school and back to my house on the hill.

My stomach does a jump-flip. And just as she's about to speak, I barf all over her. I'm burnt banana bread!

Chapter 5

I vomited all over Mrs. Rogers! Chunks of pineapple and strawberry waffles are slipping and sliding their way down her face.

Izzy laughs so loud, it rings in my ears, like when my mom tries to play piano. The sound is all bent and crooked and sharp.

Mrs. Rogers isn't wiping the vomit off her face. Instead, she turns, in a red rage, toward Izzy and picks her up as if she weighs no more than a Christmas beetle and glues her to the ceiling. Yep, that's right. She glues her to the ceiling.

Well, I don't know if she glues her or not. But I know what I'm seeing. She reaches out and puts her up all the way to the ceiling—now you get the picture of just how tall Mrs. Rogers really is—and sticks her there.

Izzy is quiet now. Well, sort of. She's still letting a giggle or two escape. And she doesn't seem worried about being stuck. I get the feeling she's been put there before.

With vomit still dripping from her face, Mrs. Rogers turns to Mr. Sanders next. He's slowly sneaking toward the door, but she marches toward him and shoves something into his mouth. Like a piece of candy or something. He suddenly thrusts his fist into the sky and calls out, "Life is great!"

Then Mrs. Rogers turns to face the class and starts speaking gibberish. *"Yoomba, loomba, tuck and tick, flow fowl pimples, flow and trick. Dukker, dooker, spooker, speak!"*

If it's a spell, it ain't one I've ever heard. But as soon as she finishes, all the students turn as white as the first full moon of the year. They each slowly speak in turn. And ever so politely.

"We were voting in Evie."

"For class president," says another.

"We love her," says Round Boy.

"She's inspirational," says Todd.

"We're sorry we were noisy," says Monique.

Mr. Sanders is singing "Everything is Awesome" into the chalkboard duster.

Izzy's lips are moving, but no words are coming out.

And me? I'm just taking it all in. Why did I think normal school would be normal? This is anything but normal. Stuff like this doesn't happen in any of the princess books I've read. And definitely nothing this exciting ever happens at my witch school. This place is even better than normal. It's cool!

Mrs. Rogers shakes her head, like she's trying to unfurl her tightly wound bun. She finally wipes what's left of my waffle vomit from her face and relaxes her long monkey-like arms. She shrinks a few sizes, and her gym suit relaxes on her body. She smiles with sickly sweetness. "Why didn't you say so? What a wonderful idea. Yes. Yes! Let's not bother voting for school president this year. Evie will be the school president. She's the perfect choice."

Her nostril hairs crawl back up her nose, and her warts shrink back into her face. She places Izzy back into her chair. And pops a candy into her mouth. Izzy spits it out and crosses her arms.

Mrs. Rogers raises her hand to Izzy. I think she might slap her. But instead, she catches a fly and shoves it into her own mouth. So gross!

"Why was Mr. Sanders cross-eyed? Because he couldn't control his pupils," says Mrs. Rogers in between crunching noises. She starts laughing like a hyena in tight polka-dot underwear.

The class all laugh. Forced. Fear-struck. Frantic.

She crunches her way to the door, turns her back to the class, and waltzes out with a fresh spring in her step.

Mr. Sanders stops singing, I'm pleased to report, and finally starts to teach us something useful—math. No witch ever believes me when I say you need a normal education. They think math and English are useless subjects. But I think they're great.

I try to forget everything that just happened, but the buzzing feeling inside my ribs won't settle down. I'm going to be school president! If that doesn't say "fitting in and fabulous," then I don't know what does.

The bell rings. It's taken me thirty minutes to do one sum. Aren't I clever?

Gertrude, Monique, and Sandy glide to my desk. "Come hang with us," says Monique.

"Sure."

We walk into the corridor together and a group of what look like kindergarteners holds up one of my party flyers.

"Can you sign this for me?" says a little boy in the group.

"Um. Yes. Sure. I suppose. I guess. Yes, of course." I'm stuttering again. I haven't practiced signing my name before, but I try my best. Evie Everyday does sound like someone famous, right? Like a leader. School president today, national president tomorrow.

"Are we allowed to come to your party?" says the little girl beside him.

Before I can answer with a jolly yes, Sandy

flicks her brown hair over her shoulder, grabs the flyer I'm signing, and shoves it at the poor kindergartener. "No little kids allowed. Buzz off!" The five little kids run off, looking terrified.

As I look around, I notice everyone has one of my party flyers. And I mean everyone. How did Monique pass them out so quickly? Kids are waving at me. I wave back. Another kid taps me on the shoulder. "Do you have any more popcorn?"

"No," I say, remembering I forgot to collect my friends from Mrs. Rogers. Nip will be especially mad at me. "Hey, I'll see you guys later. I need to get something from Principal Rogers."

"We'll come with you," says Gertrude, clinging to my arm.

I knock on the door with an equal mixture of fear and excitement churning together in my stomach.

"Just go in," says Sandy.

"Mrs. Rogers won't be happy if you do that," says Monique.

I listen to them arguing, then decide I'm going to go in and get my bag. I'm school president after all. I can do what I like.

"We'll keep a look out for you," says Gertrude.

I step inside the office by myself. My heart thumps to the beat of my steps, slow and steady. Bermuda! Mrs. Rogers isn't here. I'm all alone in her office.

I close the door behind me, glad that I have my friends outside. I peer inside Mrs. Rogers' drawers, cupboards, and filing cabinets. Not only is my bag nowhere in sight, but they're all empty. Empty!

I lie on the desk to gather my thoughts. The door opens. "Is she coming?" I ask, springing from the desk the way Nip springs from water.

"Miss Everyday!" a horribly familiar voice exclaims.

Oh no, it's her! It's Mrs. Rogers. And not the slightest warning from my so-called friends! They didn't even warn me. I stand as stiff as a zombie, all the life draining from my feet into the black floor.

"I was just here . . . to . . . collect . . . my school president badge," I lie just in time. Thank you, brain, thank you.

Mrs. Rogers looks chirpy and relaxed. She doesn't seem to care that I was lying on her desk. But this room is empty, so why would she? It's not like I could have stolen anything. Or gotten my stuff back. A shiver creeps up my spine. Where is my stuff? My friends, my pets, my things?

"I want to talk to you about something. Something very important," she says.

"Talk to me?"

"About your party."

"About my party?"

"Yes, the party you're going to hold at your house on Sunday." Her voice is pink and pretty and perfumed.

"What about it?"

"May I come?"

"Really?" I breathe out and release my shoulders. "You want to come to my party?"

"Sure. It will be fun."

I want to say, "No, *you* can't come. It's a kids' party. We don't want the school principal there. What fun would that be?" But instead, I say, "Yes, you can come."

Mrs. Rogers takes me ever so softly by the arm and walks me to the door. Her black eyes look browner to me now. They're soft and kind and gentle.

"Thank you!" She opens the door and part leads, part throws me out. I skid across the linoleum and land in front of Izzy.

Chapter 6

Did Mrs. Rogers just ask me if she could come to my party? Wow, she really does like me. A lot. The school principal at Pergoria didn't even know my name. Mrs. Rogers is so thoughtful. And considerate.

I think of all she's done for me over the last two days. She's helped me fit in. She's helped me become class president. And she even wants to come to my party.

I look up at Izzy. Her usual sunshine smile is gone. She looks unhappy. Downright angry. Or depressed. I can't tell which.

"What's up?" I say.

She holds up one of my party flyers. I look at the black ink on the white paper. "Come to a cool party on the hill," I read. "It's not haunted in the slightest, and only awesome kids are allowed to attend."

The flyer seems pretty clear to me. But then my eyes scroll down to the last sentence. Also because Izzy is pointing at it. It says, "Izzy is not allowed to come, so please don't tell her." Oops.

I forgot I wrote that. I gulp down my guilt.

"Oh, that. Well, you see, it's a black-clothes-only party. You understand, right? Now that I'm the school president and everything. And Mrs. Rogers is coming."

I watch Izzy's face change from unhappy, angry, depressed to miserable, raging, furious. She rips the paper into tiny pieces and throws them at my face.

"I always thought witches were kind and funny and super amazing. But you, Evie, are mean and horrid. I wouldn't come to your party even if you were a queen and personally invited me. I hate you!"

She runs down the corridor, and I realize I have an audience. Kids start clapping. Todd comes and helps me off the floor. "You're so wonderful," he says in a blank voice.

I push away the tightness in my chest

and wish I could go back in time and do that differently. But I can't.

I stick my hands in my pockets and shuffle down the corridor. What's the matter with me? I got what I wanted, right? No Izzy. I push her out of my brain. I have a perfect party to plan.

I walk through my house. I feel pleased and proud of how I managed to transform it. And it was no easy job. I do feel a teensy-weensy bit bad for using magic. But I had no choice. There was no other way of changing all the colorful, crazy stuff in my house into simple, elegant black furniture. And there was no way to get Winston, the piano, out of the house without magic. He's huge and uncooperative and would have played happy music all night if I had let him stay.

Are you wondering where my parents are?

I chickened out of telling them about the party. Instead, I begged, and I mean begged, my Auntie Floss to invite them to her place for the day. She's the only person I can really confide in.

She lives in South Africa, so it's a big trip. It takes about four hours on broomstick.
I pretended I was sick. Once they were gone, it took a couple of hours for me to conjure up some cucumber sandwiches, turn all the furniture black, and make the building look posh and polished. Which is really weird. It should normally take me about twenty minutes.

Kids are arriving. I see Monique, Sandy, and Gertrude. Is that Mrs. Parker, the town snoop hiding behind the shrub?

"Hey, Monique. Hi, Sandy. Hey, Gertrude. Thanks for coming."

"Your place is amazing. It was worth walking through the cemetery to get here," says Sandy.

"Are there definitely no zombies inside?" says Gertrude.

"Go look for yourself."

I sneak up behind Mrs. Parker.

"Hi, Mrs. Parker. Would you like to come to my party? Mrs. Rogers is coming."

Mrs. Parker straightens her black skirt and top and coughs. "I don't think so."

"There's cucumber sandwiches."

"Oh, really? Are your parents around? The house looks very different." She wanders inside the house.

"Hi, Rick. Hey, Brenda. What's up, Todd?" More kids from school are arriving.

"I can't believe it. Your house has completely changed." Mrs. Parker is looking at me with her spy eyes.

"But you haven't been here before, have you?" I say, knowing full well she has. But she won't dare admit it.

"No, no, of course not."

Mrs. Rogers comes through the front door. She's wearing a tight black dress and matching headpiece. She looks exactly like Maleficent now. The only thing she's missing is the horns.

"Ruth. What are you doing here?" she says to Mrs. Parker.

"I was just leaving," says Mrs. Parker. She looks scared.

"Do stay. No need to hurry away."

But Mrs. Parker yells out of nowhere and runs down the hill like the house came to life again. It didn't, so I have no idea what's with that.

Mrs. Rogers shrugs her shoulders and turns back to me. "What a good job you've done with this party, Evie. Are your parents home?" Her voice is sweet and kind and dripping with delight.

I start fidgeting with my dress. "They had to

go out. Urgent business. They'll be back later."

"Oh, good, good." Mrs. Rogers's face is all twisted and deformed as she says this, but I don't have time to wonder why because someone's put loud music on and the dancing starts. I wait for Mrs. Rogers to yell at everyone to stop dancing, but instead she joins in.

We dance. We eat cucumber sandwiches. We sit around on the black furniture. The party is a complete success.

Mrs. Rogers stops the music and gives a speech about how wonderful I am and how lucky the town is to have me. Everything is going amazing. I'm really, totally normal now. I fit in. It's true. I'm not Evie Everyday Witch anymore. I'm Evie Everyday girl. Nothing could ruin my normal, perfect life. Nothing.

Everyone's cheering for me again. It's been a big week of cheers. Then I see her. Izzy. She's outside, staring at me with big cat eyes. I need to get rid of her before Mrs. Rogers sees her and thinks I've invited her.

"Thank you all so much," I say as the cheering dies down.

I tense, debating whether I risk using magic. Not to mention it isn't working like usual anyway. And I'm trying really hard not to use magic, remember? But what else am I supposed to do? I chant the magic words, softly, so I don't feel so bad for cheating, and breathe with relief when everyone goes back to dancing. It worked!

I storm outside. "What are you doing here? I'm sorry, but even though you dress brilliantly"— she's wearing a turquoise dress with bright orange polka dots that is absolutely stunning— "and you're fun, and always happy, and cook amazing breakfasts, I can't be your friend!"

Izzy's upside-down mouth turns back up again. She grins at me, then throws herself on me, hugging me tight. "You do like me. You are my friend." She pulls away and holds my backpack toward me. My original bright pink backpack. "Look what I found for you."

I look without touching it.

"Aren't you excited? It's your stuff. Your cat, your bat, your corncob."

How does she know about my cat and bat and corncob? My eyes glaze over and I feel dizzy.

"I told you, I know you're a witch. And I'm sick and tired of you pretending you're not. This town needs you. You have to do something about all this." She waves her spare hand toward my house and party.

I feel a storm brewing inside my chest. "What do you mean? This is perfect. I'm totally normal and everyone loves me. For the first time in my life I fit in."

"But your life was perfect before. You already had everything you wanted."

"You don't know anything about my life. I was miserable before I came here. I'm popular for the first time ever and I'm not going to let you take that away from me."

Izzy reaches for my hand. "Evie. This isn't you. This isn't real. They don't like you. They've been tricked."

I pull my hand away and calm my breathing.

How dare she? I push back my tears and speak slowly at first, then pick up speed. "I'm happy for the first time ever and you're trying to ruin it. You're jealous. That's what you are. You're a horrible, jealous BRAT!"

Izzy drops her shoulders, her smile, and my bag, and runs down the hill at top speed.

My head starts hurting and my body feels heavy. I look at my bag through blurred vision. I am happy. Aren't I?

I lean slowly toward my bag. A cuddle with Nip will make me feel better.

But I feel a hand grab mine before I can pick it up. Mrs. Rogers. Her voice is all light and bubbly. "You don't need those things anymore, Evie. You fit in now. You're one of us. You don't want to go back, do you?"

"Go back? No. No! I don't want to go back. I'm normal."

"Yes, you are, dear. Let's keep it that way."

I walk back in, half dazed. I'm happy. Everything has gone my way. Life is perfect. Life is totally normal.

But my mind thinks only of Izzy.

Chapter 7

I walk up the steps of Wyndemere. The orange bricks seem to glow today. My steps are heavy. Why do I feel like this when I had the best party ever? Kids are high-fiving me the whole way to class.

"Best party ever!"

"Love your house."

"You're so normal."

I'm finally a Lamron—normal spelled backward, remember—and it feels . . . okay. I glide into my classroom. I have the glide down pat now. I've been practicing every minute I get.

Izzy's in the front row, wearing sunglasses. She looks the other way. She's wearing a vanilla-colored dress with bright, colorful balloons painted all over it. Just to torment me, I guess.

My mind races and I bite my lip. My bag is on my desk. Not the black one I've been bringing to school every day. My pink bag with polka dots all over it. The one Izzy brought to my party. The one I left on my lawn with Mrs. Rogers. I look over at Izzy again, but she's got her back turned to me. Did she do this?

"Take your seats, everyone. This morning, we're going to have a science pop quiz." Mr. Sanders looks bright and chirpy.

Science? I don't know anything about science.

I give in to the temptation to look inside my bag. I haven't seen my friends for a week. The first thing I pull out is Sylvie. My bat. She's still in the shape of glasses.

"Evie, what is the center of a cell called?" says Mr. Sanders.

I haven't got a clue. But I bet Sylvie does. I put my Sylvie glasses on my face. And I see the answer as clear as day.

"A nucleus."

"Well done, Evie."

My glasses wobble around on my face. Sylvie's happy to see me.

"Todd, what is the most powerful part of a tornado? Is it underneath the tornado, along the sides, high above, or the center?"

Todd looks out the window as if a tornado might come by and help him out with the answer. "The center?"

"Good try, Todd. Not quite right. Anyone else want to have a go?"

I stick my hand up so high I feel my shoulder

pop.

"Evie."

"Along the sides."

For some reason, everyone is glaring at me.
It's not my fault I'm smart. Well, I'm not really
smart, but Sylvie is. I look at Mr. Sanders and
see an image of a white cat crawling around him.
Sylvie sees stuff, remember?

"I didn't know you had a white cat called
Rosie, Mr. Sanders," I say.

"How do you know that?" He shakes his
head, and lucky for me, moves back to the
pop quiz. "Izzy, what's another word for water
power?"

Izzy mumbles something I can't hear. She's
not at all herself. I guess she's mad at me for
calling her jealous. Sylvie shows me tears
glistening under Izzy's glasses. Sheesh!

"Not sure what that answer is. Anyone else?"

says Mr. Sanders.

I shoot my hand up.

"Evie . . . again," he says.

The class makes their *muh* sheep noise. The one they make when they're not happy.

"Hydropower!"

"Well done. You know an awful lot about science. Monique, you can answer this next question. What do we call materials that harm living things by interfering with life processes?"

Monique looks under her desk, then at Gertrude and Sandy. Then finally at me. I ignore her pleading stare, stick up my hand, and yell, "Pollutants."

The class *muhs* at me again. Monique shoots me a death stare. One kid even boos. What's the matter? Isn't it cool to be smart at this school? I'm the school president. The girl who threw the coolest party ever.

I want to answer the next question wrong to make the kids in my class happy, but the right answer is so hard to resist. After I answer all fifty questions by myself, we move onto math.

One kid throws scrunched-up paper at me. Another shoots spitballs at me. Lots of them land on my glasses. Sylvie starts wiggling back and forth like crazy. She is being attacked, after all. And just like that, she turns, in plain sight, back into a bat!

She flies toward Mr. Sanders, who starts screaming, and then she whizzes around the room so fast it's all a blur.

There's lots of screaming, and I'm being pushed and shoved. Everyone is freaking out. It's just a bat, for goodness' sake. I take a deep breath and blink my eyes several times until I can see clearly again.

Sylvie is making nose dives at kids' faces.

She's on the attack. Todd is banging on the
classroom door as though it's locked and there's
no escape from this horror movie. Monique and
Sandy are both under their desks. Gertrude
swats at Sylvie with a book. And Izzy? Izzy is
sitting at her desk, sunglasses on, and doesn't
seem to care one bit.

"Stop, Sylvie. Stop!" I yell. And just like that, Sylvie turns back into a pair of glasses and lands square in the middle of my desk.

Some kids are crying. Some are still screaming. But all of them are staring at me. Mr. Sanders too. Everyone but Izzy.

"You are a witch."

Don't ask me who said that. I'm too upset to notice.

"You're not normal at all." That was Round Boy.

I grab my bag and Sylvie, and run, crying, from the room. I run all the way home to the top of the hill. I run into my room and hide under my covers. There's no way I'm taking Sylvie to school with me tomorrow!

Chapter 8

I walk up the steps of Wyndemere, a little terrified and a lot scared.

"Hey, Evie!" says Todd. He sounds happy and nice and friendly. Maybe a pair of glasses turning into a bat in class isn't so weird after all.

Monique glides up to me. "Can I have a turn with your magical glasses?"

Before I can answer, Gertrude and Sandy rush up and hug me like I'm still their favorite person.

"Us too," says Sandy.

"It's not a real bat, is it?" says Gertrude.

"No, of course not. It was just a trick I learned from the TV. A magic trick," I lie.

"It did look like a real bat," says Monique.

"Especially when it dived at us. Your trick was chillin'," says Gertrude.

"Do you have them?" says Monique.

"I didn't bring my bag to school today. Not that bag anyway." I hold up my nice black bag. I left the other one at home. On purpose.

"Promise you'll bring them tomorrow?" says Sandy.

"Sure."

All four of us walk arm in arm to class. As we enter the room, Izzy stares up at me with sunglasses still on her face. She's wearing a red jumpsuit with pale pink hearts all over it. Even when she's angry her dress style is on point. She's so mean, honestly. So mean.

I huff at her. I don't care what she thinks.

I have friends, and she doesn't. I high-five Monique, Sandy, and Gertrude.

Then I spot it on my desk. I freeze and run my hands through my knotty hair. It's my pink backpack. It's returned. It's here. Again! I'm absolutely positive I left it at home, but here it is. I rub my eyes in case I'm seeing things.

When I open them again, it's still there. I start breathing through my nostrils, all huffy and puffy like a cat who's been slapped on the end of a witch's broom. Cats are scared of heights in case you didn't know.

"I thought you said you didn't bring your bag today?" says Monique.

"You didn't have to lie if you don't want to share your glasses with us," says Gertrude.

Sandy flicks her hair in my face. "How rude!"

I collapse into my chair. I reach into my bag and pull out Nip. He's still a diary, poor thing, and hasn't said a single word to me. I look around to make sure no one is watching me. I lean in close. "*Psst.* Nip. How did you get here?"

Nothing. He's madder than I guessed. Not sure why. He's a diary, so he doesn't have to eat or poop. He doesn't need company. What's his problem?

"Nip, say something. I'm sorry, Okay. Nip? Nip!" I poke his deep purple fur cover. No reply.

"Mr. Sanders, Evie is talking to her diary," says Todd as Mr. Sanders walks into the classroom.

"I don't see what's wrong with that. Girls love to write in diaries. Right, girls?"

"*Muh!*" These kids are nothing more than sheep, I tell you.

"No!" says Todd. "She's not writing in her diary. She's talking to it. She keeps calling out Nip!"

I shove the diary behind my back. Mr. Sanders gives me an is-this-true stare.

I shake my head from side to side. I feel the diary slip from my fingers. Round Boy manages to get up from his seat next to Izzy and grab it before me. He must still have a grudge at me for kicking him and taking his seat. Who can blame him?

He waves the diary above his head, and

starts doing laps around the classroom. Around all the desks. Around Mr. Sanders. He throws Nip into the air and catches him like a panther playing with its prey. Round Boy has a look of madness on his face. He's flipped the witch's hat, he has. He's as mad as a witch whose broom's been stolen.

I want to chase him. To yell at him to stop. But I'm frozen. My black sneakers feel glued to the floor. My black dress glued to the chair. My tongue glued to the roof of my mouth.

What could possibly happen?, I ask myself. Mr. Sanders will eventually catch him and make him give Nip back. Everything is going to be fine. And I'll think up a good punishment for Round Boy. I am school president after all.

The diary goes flying up into the air again and again. My poor dizzy, dazed diary. Poor Nip!

The diary starts growling and then Nip speaks. Out loud! "I will bite you so hard you're going to yell like a hound dog!"

Round Boy steps back and looks around for who said that. Everyone gasps. The diary falls with a splat on the floor.

Please no, please no, please no, I chant in my head. But I still can't move. I feel hot. Boiling. Feverish.

The diary starts moving and cursing. I don't want to tell you the words it's saying, as they're rude. Really rude!

Mr. Sanders tenses his shoulders, furrows his eyebrows, and points his finger at Nip. "Stop that, you rude little diary."

One third of the class is giggling at Mr. Sanders telling off a diary. Another third is looking at the diary and wondering what's happening. And the last third is looking at me. Looking at me in a not-nice way.

The diary morphs into a purple pumpkin, then into a purple cauldron, and finally into a purple cat. Didn't I mention Nip is purple?

"No!" I scream, finally forcing myself to move. I grab at Nip, but I'm too slow.

He jumps like a cricket from one desk to the other. "You rotten little weasels. This school is rotten to the core. And all you children are rotten too," he says, gritting his teeth.

No one moves. Except me. I try again to catch him, but he turns to me next. "And you, Evie. You're the worst of them all. I have sat back and done nothing while you try to fit in with these losers. But enough is enough. You are not normal. You are a—"

I jump on him, shove my whole hand in his big mouth, and mutter the magic words under my breath. It doesn't work! He's still a cat. What's happening to me? What's happening to this class? One minute they love me, then they don't. One minute they're like sheep, then they're wild and untamable. Something isn't right.

I close my eyes tight and try again with the magic words. Phew! This time they work. He turns back into a diary and sits in my hands, hissing. I poke him and he stops. I take in a big breath of air and smile at everyone's horrified faces.

"This is nothing. Just magic. From TV. I learned how to do that last night. Cool, right? I'm so cool. I'm normal. I'm—"

"Weird!" says Monique.

"Very strange!" says Mr. Sanders.

I sniffle back my tears.

Izzy takes off her sunglasses and gives me a small smile. Just a small one, but a smile nonetheless. No one else is looking at me. No one.

I sit back at my desk and shove Nip back into my bag, glad that ordeal is over. Glad for whatever reason Mrs. Roger's hasn't turned up.

There's a tickling sensation on my fingers. The tickling is getting stronger and stronger, and then I smell it. Popcorn. Hot, fresh popcorn. As it erupts from my bag with a *pop*, everyone starts clapping. They reach out their hands for popcorn and stuff it into their mouths like they didn't have any breakfast.

Mr. Sanders is yelling over the sound of corn popping. "Enough! Evie, go to the principal's office. Now!"

Pops trembles his way out of my bag, shaking and wobbling on his two little green legs. His brown kernel eyes are double their usual size, and he starts running around the room like an insect running away from a hungry bird. This time, the kids start laughing and chasing him. Poor Pops is so terrified he starts popping corn even faster! He shoots corn around the room like a witch's spell gone wrong, and soon the entire floor is covered in so much popcorn, no one can move.

I dive across the room, pretending I'm riding my broom in the state witch's championship, and get ahold of that crazy, sensitive corncob. I squeeze him tight in my hands. He finally stops popping. I catch Izzy smiling at me again.

I give her the meanest, scariest witch face I can make. She did this. She brought my bag to school again. She's determined to ruin my life. I poke my tongue out at her and turn my head away.

Mr. Sanders decides it's punishment enough for me to clean up all the popcorn. It takes me thirty-five trips to the trash to cart it all out. Monique, Gertrude, and Sandy won't look at me the whole time. Todd is making faces at me. And Round Boy is laughing. At me!

Another failed day of school. This is getting out of hand. I pledge to tie my bag to my bed tomorrow. I can still get this back on track. I am a Lamron. No one and nothing is going to ruin this for me.

Chapter 9

I've turned over a new leaf. Instead of lying to be
liked, today I'm bribing them. With chocolate chip
cookies. Everyone here loves cookies. Luckily
for me, Izzy is absent today so there's no chance
of my pink bag showing up at school. That and I
chained it to the tree outside my bedroom.

I decide I'd better include Mrs. Rogers in my
bribery plan. I'm sure she'd love a cookie. And
it will give me a chance to check if she's heard
the rumors about bats, cats, and corn popping in
class.

I knock on her door, both my hands clenched

tight around my cookie tin.

"Come in."

I walk in slowly. Carefully. I don't know what mood she's in yet, and whether she's on my side. Is that my white wand shining back at me from her black desk? She sits on it suddenly and does a yoga pose or something. Weird.

"Be quick. I have things to do," she snaps.

"I wondered if you want a cookie. They're chocolate chip."

"No, I don't want a stupid cookie. Get out. I have spells to cast," she says gruffly. "I mean, papers to correct." Her tone is syrupy now.

I pop my ears. I'm hearing things. I'm under a lot more stress than I thought.

She's shoving something down her back. Not my wand, I'm sure. She wouldn't have taken it. She's on my side. Everything was in my bag, wasn't it? I'm so mad at myself for not checking it properly. I decide to ask her.

"Is that my wand? I mean, my ordinary white stick?" Oops.

"Your wand? No. I don't know what you're talking about," she says with glee. But then she blurts out, "I'm going to take all your powers and turn you into a tree!"

I must be hearing things again. Mrs. Rogers covers her mouth with both her hands. It looks like some invisible force is pulling her hands away, and she's slapping herself, trying to resist.

That's when I remember. My wand! It's my white wand. I have two, a white one and a black one, remember? The white one makes you tell the truth. Especially if you're touching it.

"Give me my wand!" I demand.

"No, you rotten little good-for-nothing witch!"

I'm hot all of a sudden. The springs in my brain *boing* again, rusty and raging and looking for answers. Does Mrs. Rogers think I'm a witch because of the bat and the cat and corn? Or has she always known?

"I'm not a witch. I'm just a girl. You're on my side, right?"

"Yes, Evie. You're normal," she says calmly. Then she's twitching her head madly and screeching, "You are a witch. I've always known it!"

I shake my head, and my voice trembles. "You knew? You won't tell anyone, will you? You're still helping me?"

"Yes," she says sweetly. "No!" she yells. "Yes. No! Yes. No!"

It's like she's gone berserk. I breathe all the way to my ribs. I know what I have to do. I calm my churning stomach and run at her like a bat rushing for the Christmas pudding. Yep, bats have a thing for Christmas pudding, don't ask me why. I knock her off the table in one try and stand up, triumphant.

Mrs. Rogers looks a bit dazed, and that's

when I see the wand on the floor beside her. I lunge for it. Just as my hands touch it, she grabs it too.

We're having a tug-of-war. Have I mentioned we witches are especially fond of tug-of-war? It's true. It's one of our favorite games. And it's the most popular game at Pergoria.

So there's no chance Mrs. Rogers is going to win. This wand is small, however, and she does have giant eagle hands. Come to think of it, how did I not notice her giant eagle hands? Her nails make claws look like they've been manicured. Even her skin looks scaled and slimy.

But there's one other thing witches are particularly good at. Cheating. I take the opportunity to sneeze on Mrs. Rogers, right in her face. I don't really sneeze, but I'm super good at pretend sneezing and convincing my parents I'm sick. You know, for when I want to take days off school. Or throw a party.

It does the trick. Mrs. Rogers lets go of the wand. I hold it up, elated and exhausted. I take three careful steps toward the door. I open it, run through, slamming it behind me, and make a dash for my classroom.

I hit the door of my classroom headfirst. Ouch! That really hurt.

Then I realize I have my eyes closed. Oops. I shake out my body and calm myself down, stick my wand under my armpit, and glide inside.

Mrs. Rogers is in my classroom, as calm as cat poo, standing right next to Mr. Sanders. How did she get here so fast? How did she get here before me?

My legs start jerking like they're scared, my hands spring to my neck like they're giving up, and the rest of my body starts vibrating like my Uncle Marty's table. He's a professional witch masseur. What? Witches get tense, too, you know.

I expect Mrs. Rogers to demand the wand, but instead she says, "Take a seat, Evie. I was just leaving."

She's going? She's giving up just like that? She's keeping my secret?

"We're still friends," she says. I'm glad she's not a sore loser.

I sit down in my chair, relieved to see the back of her.

I look at Mr. Sanders, then at the rest of the students in the class. They're all dazed, eyes glazed over. What's going on? They're in sheep mode again.

Mrs. Rogers has done something. Something not good. Something bad. I wish Izzy was here. But she's not. And that's my fault too. Everything feels like it's my fault right now. I push back my tears, and realize my pink bag is on my desk. It's on my desk again!

I push Mrs. Rogers weird behavior out of my head. I push the pain of hurting Izzy out of my heart. And I push the feeling that something is not right with the class today out of my gut.

Mr. Sanders looks green again. Not the same green as he usually looks. This green is more glowing and pale, like a freshly plucked four-leaf clover. He hasn't said a word since I came in.

"Is everything all right, Mr. Sanders?" I ask.

"*Ribbit*," he says. He sounds just like a frog about to lay eggs. Don't ask me how I know that.

"*Ribbit*," says Todd.

"*Ribbit*," says Sandy.

"*Ribbit*."

"*Ribbit*."

"*Ribbit*."

A chill creeps up my spine, and a sour taste

floods my mouth. Everyone starts to shrink. Not just shrink, but turn green and slimy too. They're all turning into frogs!

Within a minute, they're jumping and jittering and jostling all about the room. I'm not joking.

I do what any witch would do under the circumstances. I hold up my white wand and say the magic words. "*Flim flam flu. Zip zoom, bada boom. Cackle, crackle, boo. Back to Lamrons, all of you!"*

I didn't need to say that last sentence, but I think it sounded kind of cool. Don't you agree?

But nothing happens. What's wrong with my wand? What's wrong with my magic? I try again, yelling the spell louder. *"Flim flam flu. Zip zoom, bada boom. Cackle, crackle, boo!"*

Luckily it works. And just like that, they're all normal again. Todd looks right at me and points. His hair is still partly green. I can see a vein in his head twitching madly. "She just turned us into frogs. She *is* a witch!"

I collapse into my chair, too tired to stutter. Too tired to speak. Too tired to explain.

"Evie is a witch. It's true!" says Monique as she flicks out her tongue and snatches a mosquito from midflight. She screams. "You did this to us!"

"Evie is a witch. Evie is a witch. Evie is a witch," chants Mr. Sanders, while clapping his hands together like a three-year-old. He's the only person in the room who seems excited by the idea. Everyone else looks angry.

"Look! She's holding a wand. She's a witch!" says Gertrude, like she's the one who just figured it out.

They run at me. Headfirst, like they're determined to burn me at the stake. I don't feel like I have much of a choice. I point my wand at myself, say the magic words, and pray this will work the first time. I vanish. Well, I don't vanish. I just vanish from there. From school. From that place I loved. And just lost. The first place I finally fitted in.

I lie down on my bed, glad to be safe at home, and wonder how it all went wrong. I can't go back to school. Not ever. Mrs. Rogers, the students, even Mr. Sanders all think I'm a witch. They all *know* I'm a witch. My secret is out.

No more being normal for me. I've ruined everything. I let the tears drip down my face and onto my lonely black dress. It's all over.

Chapter 10

My plan to fit in and be normal has failed miserably. What went wrong? I did everything right. I wore black, lied, became school president, and threw the best party ever. All that for nothing.

Now everyone knows I'm a witch. There's no convincing them otherwise because the whole class thinks I turned them into frogs. I let a giggle escape as I remember them all croaking and hopping around the class. It was funny.

I only wish Izzy had been there to see it all. *Izzy*. She would have been on my side. She would have helped me. The guilt swirls in my stomach as I remember how mean I was to her.

I hear the doorbell. It's a witch cackle that gets louder and louder and ends in an explosion. I love that cuckoo crazy doorbell!

Winston, the piano, starts playing horror music. He never does that. Who's at the door? Mrs. Rogers, I guess.

I race there before my mom or dad. I open the door and drop my mug, my fairy bread, and my jaw. It's Izzy. And she's wearing green today. Green! My second favorite color after pink.

"I'm here to give you this." She shoves my bag into my hands. My bag! Once again, I've been a rotten friend to Sylvie, Nip, Pops, and most of all, Izzy. I see it all now, as clear as a crystal ball.

"You're a good friend. Where did you find it? How have you been getting my bag? It was you, right?"

"It wasn't me. It was Mrs. Rogers bringing it to school every day. I'm not your friend." Izzy drops my bag, turns and starts walking away. Actually, she runs. Faster than a witch on a broomstick, all the way down the hill.

I stare at the ground, hoping it loses gravity and I float to the moon. It serves me right. Why should she be my friend after all I've done?

"You're not going to let her go, are you?" says Nip in his deep, calming voice.

I pull him out of my bag. "*Flim flam flu. Zip zoom, bada boom. Cackle, crackle, boo.*" Nothing happens. What's wrong with my magic? I try again and still nothing. Third time's a charm. He's back to his cuddly cat self.

"I was a diary for over a week," says Nip, hissing at me. "We were captives to that horrible harpy. She buried us in a hole in the schoolyard!

And you did nothing."

"A harpy?" My face must look like there really is no gravity, all saggy and droopy. "That's not true!"

"It is true. Mrs. Rogers is a harpy. But you were so obsessed with being normal and popular, you didn't notice."

My brain does a complete turn, races at lightning speed, and deep dives into my memories. Mrs. Rogers's obsession with tight black gym gear. Her bun. Her unusually sharp teeth and nails.

"She can't be a harpy. She doesn't have wings!"

Nip yawns and stretches, then lounges on the pink fluffy doormat and licks his purple fur. "She does have wings."

"I would have seen them."

"You never looked at her with Sylvie. That's

why she took us from you. She knew exactly what she was doing."

"But Izzy said she gave you back to me."

Nip yawns like I'm stupid. "She gave us back on purpose to get the class to hate you. Don't you think it's weird they loved you one moment and hated you the next. It's all part of her horrible plan. You fell for it, Evie."

I feel hot. Horrible. Horrendous. Mrs. Rogers is a harpy, and I didn't see it. I was blind. And stupid. And blind! I was tricked the whole time.

"Who rescued you?" I ask, pushing away the

knot in my stomach. It wasn't me. It should have been, but it wasn't. I really, really, really let my friends down.

Before Nip can answer, I know exactly who. The only person who's been trying to help me all along. The one person who accepts me for who I am. Izzy!

I grab my yellow bristly broomstick and jump on. I grab Nip and stick him on the broom's edge. He yowls the way worms do when they're added to a witch's spell. Cats hate flying, remember? But I need Nip with me for courage. I fly into the blue sky, determined to find Izzy. I need to make this right.

I spot her picking wild flowers in the cemetery. I swoop down, just avoiding the large statue of a man pointing his finger into the sky, and do a perfect swish landing. Except Nip rolls off into the weeds growing wild around the

graves. "Sorry, Nip!"

"What do *you* want?" says Izzy. She throws her flowers onto the ground and is about to run again.

I swish my hands and force her to freeze. It's mean of me, but I don't know how else to stop her running. That girl can really run fast.

I look into her face, which is stuck in an I-hate-you expression, and pour my heart out. "I'm so, so, soooo sorry. I was wrong in every way. And you were right. I'm a nasty, rotten friend. And you have every reason to hate me. I'm awful, bad, beastly, hideous, horrid, dreadful, disturbing, and downright mean. You helped me all along, and I treated you badly."

I take my first breath in, sucking hard. "You're right, I am a witch, and instead of being proud of it, I tried to escape it. I was wrong. I wanted to be normal so much that I didn't see my only true friend. You!" I wave my hands to unfreeze Izzy and collapse next to Nip in the weeds.

"Well done," says Nip, blinking his eyes at me with love. He rubs himself on my legs.

I don't bother holding back my big tear drops. They land with a giant KERPLUNK!

I feel arms wrap around me and hands wipe away my tears. It's Izzy.

"You're forgiven. Oh, Evie, I could never hate you. Though it was fun hearing you say sorry. You're my friend. And a real witch. I know everything about you."

What does she mean? "You know everything about me?"

"Not about you exactly, but I'm a giant fan of witches. I've been studying witches my whole life. I couldn't believe it when a real witch came to my school."

"How could you tell I was a witch, exactly?

I was pretty convincing as a normal girl."

Izzy laughs. "Not really. It's pretty obvious. Your clothes. How happy you are. People from around here aren't like that."

"Are you a witch too? Is that why you're not like the rest?"

Izzy laughs even louder. "I wish! But no. I wear this for protection."

She pulls out an amulet from around her neck. It's a circle with a cross in the middle. It's how witches protect themselves.

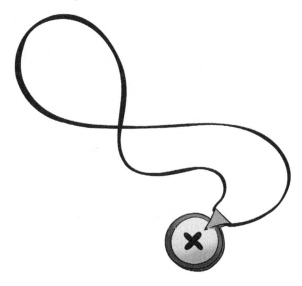

I reach my hand for mine and realize it's gone! We witches never leave the house without wearing our amulets. I was so distracted trying to fit in I don't know how long I've been without it.

"Mrs. Rogers took it from you. She's a harpy," says Izzy.

"You know about harpies? They're witches'—"

"Natural enemies." Izzy finishes my sentence. "They have giant horrid teeth, and black leathery skin, and a short stumpy horn, which Mrs. Rogers hides under her bun. And wings! She put a spell on this town a year ago, and everyone has been suffering since. Until you came." She's so excited her eyes are sparkling.

"You're not scared?"

"Nope. But I can't defeat her alone. I need your help, Evie. Together, we can beat her and save this town. Everyone's under her spell."

"Even me. I was too," I say, nudging away the

guilt wobbling in my stomach.

"But you're not now, and that's what counts."

I didn't realize how much I missed her smile until it spreads across her face. My knees start shaking again. I can't defeat a harpy. Most witches are scared to death of them. I'm scared to death of her.

"We can't beat her," I say, giving in to my fear. Give me Maleficent any day.

"Yes, we can." She pulls a small mirror from her pocket.

Izzy is a genius. And very good at research.

"The one thing harpies hate . . ." I say.

"Is a mirror!" says Izzy.

We agree to make a plan and defeat Mrs. Rogers. With Izzy by my side I convince myself it will be easy. I'm a witch, remember. Evie Everyday Witch!

Chapter 11

The warm sun is shining through my bedroom window. Izzy and I are getting ready for battle. Battle with Mrs. Rogers. We've turned Sylvie back into glasses, with an upgrade. Not only can she see useful stuff, but now she has a Mrs. Rogers supersonic-alert buzzer.

If we get close to Mrs. Rogers, Sylvie will make a noise that harpies hate. It's sonic, so humans and witches can't hear it. Neither can cats or dogs. But to harpies, it sounds like a thousand witches singing yuletide songs all at once. The sweetness and sharpness of the sound is murder to their ears.

We witches use the noise to protect ourselves from harpies all the time. It's how we keep our houses and schools safe from them.

"With these glasses and your mirrors, I think we can beat her," I say.

"Are you going to march into battle wearing black?" says Izzy. She scrunches up her nose at me like I smell.

I'm still wearing the black dress Mrs. Rogers gave me. "Why am I still wearing this?" I try to rip it off, but it won't lift over my head. No matter how hard I tug at it, it falls back down.

"Mrs. Rogers used a spell on your dress!" says Izzy. "But how have you been taking it off at night?"

I squirm my face at Izzy's words.

"You have been taking it off every night?" She laughs and squishes her nose with her fingers.

"I figured sleeping in my dress would help me love black!"

We both giggle our heads off and roll on my pink princess bed in the center of the room.

"You're so much fun, Evie. I've always dreamed of having a witch as a friend."

"Even if I'm stuck in this silly black dress forever?"

Izzy picks up a pair of scissors from my cauldron. I like to keep my school supplies in there. She tries cutting it off, but it magically stitches itself back together.

"I hope Mrs. Rogers' nose hairs crawl up her nose and into her brain and explode!" says Izzy.

"And her giant warts come to life and blast her to the moon!" I add.

"Poor moon!"

We roll around the bed again, giggling louder than ever.

"Evie, is everything all right in there?" comes my mom's voice from down the hall.

"Yep! I'm just having fun being normal!"

She opens the door and peeks in. She smiles warmly at Izzy.

"Is your friend normal or the unusual variety?"

"I've decided I'm done being normal, and I'm a witch again!" I announce.

Mom's face relaxes and I see tears in her eyes. She's happy, I'm guessing. She looks at Izzy, her face a question mark.

"Izzy's not a witch, but she's my friend," I say.

Tears start leaking from my mom's eyes. "I'm happy you found a friend. Any friend is better than none. So long as you don't hide who you are."

"Izzy knows I'm a witch, Mom. She likes me just the way I am."

My Mom looks at me like she's about to come through the door and hug me to bits, but she knows I hate that, so she resists. "Well, be good. I have to get back to work. If I don't finish this new potion by the full moon, I'll be fired. And do take the black dress off, won't you? Who wears black these days? Have fun, you two." She disappears, just as Nip slips between the door crack and into the room.

Izzy cackles as if she's a real witch. I don't blame her. Nip is wearing shiny silver armor. He's walking like a zombie on four legs.

"I'm ready for attack!" he announces.

Izzy falls back on the bed and seriously snorts as Nip pulls a long crunchy-looking carrot from his hilt and holds it forward with his paw.

"What's she laughing at?" he asks.

"You, I think. You look adorable in that costume. Where did you find it? And what's with the carrot?"

"Adorable?" He hisses at me. "Adorable? I'm vicious and violent and volatile!" Nip has a thing for *V* words.

"I'm sure you are! To rabbits!" Izzy wipes the tears of laughter from her face. "Mrs. Rogers will be terrified of the carrot. Either that or she'll choke, munching on it."

"I thought I liked you, but now I'm not so sure," says Nip. He rolls his eyes first at Izzy and then at me.

"I did save you from that hole you were buried under, remember?" Izzy scratches the back of Nip's ear with one hand and feeds him some pineapple from the fruit platter.

Nip's a freak for fruit. He goes crazy over the stuff. But Mom never lets him eat too much. It makes him fart.

He wiggles his whiskers from side to side, licking and purring in delight. "I suppose you're all right. So what is the plan?"

"We've turned Sylvie back into glasses, and given her an upgrade of harpy sonic repellent. And Izzy is ready with mirrors."

Izzy pulls out two small mirrors from the pockets in her green dress and flashes them about the room. "Super cool. She won't stand a chance against these."

"Good, good," says Nip. "What else?"

"We have you, our knight in shining armor," I say.

Nip stands on his hind legs and holds his

sword to the sky. He's one happy cat!

"And I have my wand." I hold up my white wand. I feel like one of the Musketeers. Yep, I read that book too.

Izzy pulls a twisted tropical-colored lollipop from her pocket and holds it up. We really are like the Three Musketeers.

"All for one!"

"And one for all!" answer Izzy and Nip.

It's time for Mrs. Rogers to become burnt banana bread. She won't stand a chance against us. We're invincible. All powerful. Unbeatable.

Chapter 12

We wait until everyone is in class, then duck down like ninja witches. There is such a thing, you know. Witches who know kung fu! One time, my dad tossed his broom to my Auntie Floss, and instead of catching it, she karate chopped it into tiny pieces of firewood.

She's felt bad ever since. But I'd never seen anything so cool. I'm trying to channel some of my Auntie Floss today. I can feel my knees wobbling, and my breathing sounds like a donkey flying on a broomstick. I have seen one of those, in case you think I'm making it up.

"Evie. Focus." Izzy nudges me in the back. And back to my mission. "You can do this! We can beat her."

Did I mention witches are terrified of harpies? And for good reason. A harpy can rip a witch into a million tiny pieces with their claws and eat them. Well, that's what my dad told me. My bottom lip starts trembling, and I can feel the hairs on my head joining in the fear party.

"Onward and upward!" yells Nip as he *clinks* and *clangs* loudly toward Mrs. Rogers' office. So much for a quiet entrance.

We run after him. Izzy pushes open the office door, and we rush in. I'm terrified. Totally terrified. Make that . . . really, really, *really* terrified.

Mrs. Rogers is sitting at her desk, filing her long talons. She smiles. Long, sharp, black teeth have replaced her Cinderella smile.

"Welcome. Come in, sit down." She looks

calm and happy, like she doesn't care that Nip is pointing a carrot at her or that I'm wearing Sylvie supersonic glasses on my face. Why aren't my glasses working on her?

"Now! Do it now!" I yell to Izzy.

Izzy evil-cackle laughs. What's with that? She pulls the two mirrors from her pocket and shoves them toward Mrs. Rogers' face. "Take that, you evil harpy! You're going to melt any minute now. Or explode. Or shrink into nothing."

I start clapping, preparing for her to drop dead. That's what really happens when you shine a mirror into a harpy's face. Mrs. Rogers doesn't move. She doesn't even shrink.

Instead, she stands up, spreads a pair of wings from her back, pulls out a black wand, and points it at Izzy. My black wand! The one I have at my house.

"How did you get my wand?"

"From your lovely party! *Booga bugga boom*!"

Izzy falls to the floor unconscious and drops her mirrors. Nip charges at Mrs. Rogers with his carrot. He flies through the air, like one crazy kooky cat, does a somersault, and aims the carrot right at Mrs. Rogers' face.

She darts just in time. Nip flies right past her and through the open window.

Bang! Crash! Clang! Hiss! Screech!

I don't think he had a very good landing.

It's all up to me now. I have to stop her.

I gulp so hard I think I swallowed my tonsils. I spread my legs so my knees can't find each other. I imagine I am Snow White and this is the Evil Queen. I can defeat her. I *will* defeat her.

I pull off my glasses. Are they not working on her because she has my wand? *"Flim flam flu. Zip zoom, bada boom. Cackle, crackle, boo."*

Nothing happens. My magic isn't working properly again. I shake the glasses in my hand and try again. Sylvie turns back into a bat and charges at Mrs. Rogers. She's also weeing bat pee all over her. That stuff can melt through plastic. And it burns harpies.

"Yes! Go, Sylvie!"

I fall backward in shock and disgust. Mrs. Rogers laughs so deeply, she makes the Evil

Queen seem nice and friendly. She waves her wand—I mean *my* wand—at Sylvie and turns her into a frog. How rude! She's not affected by the bat pee at all.

"I wasn't going to do this, but you give me no choice," I say.

I reach into my backpack, squeeze my hands tight around Pops, and fling him at her. Corn starts popping in Mrs. Rogers' face, and she can't resist the temptation to stuff her mouth with it. Who can blame her? Pops' corn is crazy good.

I reach for my wand and think of Mrs. Rogers turning into a pink flamingo. Don't judge me. It's the first thing that popped into my brain.

"Flim flam flu. Zip zoom, bada boom. Cackle, crackle, boo."

I'm relieved the spell works the first time around. But instead of Mrs. Rogers turning into a pink flamingo, Pops does. I hit the wrong target.

I try again, but Mrs. Rogers jumps up and my spell hits the desk instead. The two flamingos— Pops and the desk—start charging at me. My heart feels like it's jumping from my chest to my throat, to my chest to my throat, and back again. I don't know what to do!

Mrs. Rogers is laughing like a witch on Halloween morning, all happy and crazy at the same time.

I have one chance to do this next spell right, or I'm about to be a flamingo feast! I twirl my wand, ready for a double spell, and say the magic words.

Both the flamingos turn back into their normal selves. Yes!

Pops faints, and the desk lands with a thump on my foot. Ouch! I pull my foot out from under the desk, and point my white wand at Mrs. Rogers. She starts dancing around the room and points my black wand back at me.

"You can't hurt me!" she yells.

"I'm really a witch," I confess.

"Of course you are. I knew that all along. But you're not going to be a witch for very long. Your wish is coming true, Evie. You're going to be a normal girl. All your witch powers will soon be mine." She laughs low and deep, like how I imagine Santa would. I wouldn't know for sure, as I've never met Santa. You know, just like the *ho ho ho*, except *ha ha ha*.

"I don't believe you. Give me back my wand, or I'll turn you into a puddle of bat pee!"

"Ha ha ha!" She Santa Claus laughs at me again. "You can't do anything to hurt me." She flashes my talisman around her neck.

My talisman! Izzy was right. That harpy stole my wand and my necklace. "You horrid thieving harpy!"

Mrs. Rogers crosses her arms proudly. "I can hurt you, Evie. Witches don't like harpies, do they? Harpies eat witches." She makes pretend crunching noises that make me want to run from this school and never come back.

I glance at Izzy. She looks asleep on the floor.

And I think of Todd, Monique, Sandy, Gertrude, Round Boy, and all the other kids. They need me. I have to save them.

"Flim flam flu. Zip zoom, bada boom. Cackle, crackle, boo." I see the spark spit out of the tip of my white wand, head toward my black one, then double back at me. I scream. But I'm too slow. The spark hits my white wand and splits it into two.

"I won!" she yells.

I know she has, but I can't bear the thought of Mrs. Rogers taking my witch powers. "You'll never be a witch." I'm huddled next to Izzy and wondering what my bones will taste like when Mrs. Rogers takes her first bite.

She comes toward me, towering over me like a vampire ready to suck my blood. Her eyes are fire red and flashing.

"Your dress has been draining your witch

powers ever since you put it on. It won't be long now. But don't be sad. I won't kill you. I will just give you what you always wanted. You'll be normal and popular. You'll be my prize pupil."

I feel light-headed and dizzy as I see her put my flute to her lips. My flute! She took that too! I was tricked. Fooled. Hoodwinked.

I feel the last bit of fight leave me as Mrs. Rogers plays my magic flute. It hypnotizes animals, but today it's working perfectly well on Wyndemere students. Kids pour in around us like zombie children. They stare straight ahead and chant, "Evie! Evie! Evie!"

Mrs. Rogers stops playing and yells over their chanting. "Your powers are mine now, Evie, and you are a normal little girl like you've always wanted."

I wish I could puke on her again. I wish I could yell and scream and run away from this horrible normal school. I wish I had never wished to be a normal girl.

I feel tingling all over my body. Like when Nip crawls on me in the morning to wake me up. I guess it's the last bit of my magic leaving. I've failed.

Mrs. Rogers is right. I did want to be normal. And I got what I wanted.

I breathe out in defeat.

But then I spot it. Izzy's talisman. The one just like mine, around her neck. Maybe, just maybe I have enough magic left. I grab Izzy's necklace and tug as hard as I can. It snaps off her neck, and I hold the amulet in my hand tight.

"I'm proud to be a witch. I'm proud to be a witch. I'm proud to be witch," I chant under my breath.

The noise around me is deafening. I can see Round Boy right next to Mrs. Rogers. They're all chanting, "Evie, Evie, Evie." Even Mrs. Rogers. They're under her spell again.

I don't know if this will work. I imagine being my Auntie Floss, proud to be a witch and full of ninja skills. I jump to my feet, hold the talisman above my head, and scream at the top of my voice, "I am Evie Everyday Witch! *Flim flam flu. Zip zoom, bada boom. Cackle, crackle, boo.*"

At the same time, I imagine my dress turning back into my regular clothes. My glitter-speckled sneakers. My pink-and-orange striped stockings. My purple skirt and favorite green top. If there's even a little bit of magic in me, this could work.

A bright orange light glitzes across the room like when the sun is about to set. I freeze with my hand above my head, still holding the talisman tight. My fear just a heartbeat away. I pray this will work.

The other kids all freeze too. Mrs. Rogers

146

opens her eyes at least ten times wider. First, she drops my wand; then she drops my flute. Finally, her big black wings grow twice as large.

Oh no! My spell didn't work after all. I close my eyes and expect her to hit me with her wings. Harpies can use them to send you halfway around the planet with one sweep.

Instead, there's a loud shrieking sound, like one thousand bats all racing for first place in the Annual Bat-Racing Roundup. I peek between my fingers.

Mrs. Rogers is shrinking, like she's being barbecued on a hot flame. Her wings are curling up, and her face is so scrunched I can't make out her nose from her eyes. Her skin is turning red. She's shrinking right before me.

I look down and see my bright clothes are back. It worked. The black dress is gone.

Mrs. Rogers continues to shriek and squawk.

Izzy comes to, stands up, and gives me a huge
hug.

"You did it! You beat her, Evie."

I'm so relieved she's fine.

Nip crawls back through the window and sits
all straight and proud on the windowsill. "Die you
vile, vampish vixen," he hisses.

Sylvie turns back into herself and wees
all over the shrinking Mrs. Rogers for good
measure.

All that's left of her now is a ghastly black
ball. She looks like a baseball covered in tar.
I count to five, and there's a giant *pop!* Just like
that, Mrs. Rogers disappears.

"Hooray!" yell all the kids. I think they're back
to their normal selves once and for all.

I rub my eyes to make sure what I'm seeing
is real. No one is wearing black anymore.
Everyone is wearing normal, everyday clothes.

"You're a witch!" yells Round Boy. He points to my head. I reach up and see I'm wearing my witch hat. It's black with a purple sash. It's the one bit of black that witches really do wear.

Silence. Everyone stares at me. Even Nip and Izzy.

"Yes, I am. I am Evie. Evie Everyday. I am Evie Everyday, and I'm a witch!"

Silence again.

I gulp.

"Hooray!" yells Monique.

"Hooray!" they all agree.

Pops starts popping corn like crazy. Kids are throwing popcorn around the room and stomping on the spot where Mrs. Rogers had been.

The door opens. Everyone goes instantly quiet. It's Mr. Sanders.

"What's the meaning of this?" he says sternly.

"Evie defeated Mrs. Rogers!" says Izzy.

Mr. Sanders looks around the room. He doesn't seem convinced Mrs. Rogers is really gone. His mouth turns up slightly at the corners. First a little, then a lot. His shoulders relax and he lunges his head back and yells, "Hooray!"

Hooray!

Chapter 13

The next day, I tell my parents everything. How Mrs. Rogers was a harpy and how she put a spell on the whole town. And how she tricked me.

My parents didn't notice anything was wrong. Witches don't care what happens to normal people. They don't pay them any attention. But my mom and dad said they felt a "moral obligation" to do something. I think that means they feel guilty for not noticing.

Anyway, they're at a town meeting right now putting a forget-everything spell on everyone.

It will make the town forget the whole year of wearing black and being boring.

And me? It took a lot of begging, but Mom and Dad agreed I get to keep going to Wyndemere Elementary. So long as I keep practicing my spells.

It's a secret that I'm a witch again, thanks to Mom and Dad's spell, but this time around, I'm going to be myself. No more hiding who I really am. It doesn't really matter if everyone else has been spelled to forget I'm a witch. The person that matters to me the most is Izzy. She still knows who I really am. My parents agreed to let her remember, so long as she keeps it a secret. I don't think the spell would have worked on her anyway. Izzy is so determined to be herself, not even Mrs. Rogers' magic worked on her.

She's at my house today making pink frosted cupcakes with me.

"I'm so glad we can still go to school together," I say.

"Your parents are really nice."

I flick my new white wand about to ice a
cupcake, but decide the regular way would
be more fun. "Yep, they're cool. They feel bad
not noticing what was going on with me. Dad
promised to take more time off work to read with
me. And Mom said she'll help me make some
new clothes."

"You do look way better in color," says Izzy.

"I don't know how I survived so long without
my pink and orange stockings!"

Izzy smiles at me. Her teeth are covered in
pink frosting. "I'm really glad you don't want to
be normal anymore. You're the best just the way
you are. Will you teach me some magic?"

Nip's purple fur stands on end. "She will
not! That would be breaking the witches' code.
Number 209 clearly states—"

I stick a giant strawberry into Nip's mouth.
"Purr. Mmmm."

"Sure, I would love to teach you some magic. And Nip won't tell anyone. Will you, Nip?"

Nip shakes his head from side to side.

Izzy giggles.

Pops pops.

And Sylvie flies around our heads, glad to be back to her bat-like self.

And me? I'm tingling all up and down my spine. Light is bursting from my face. My feet are dancing with happiness. I'm Evie. Evie Everyday. I'm a witch. A kind, funny, smart, colorful, awesome, cool WITCH!

READY TO READ THE NEXT BOOK IN THE SERIES?

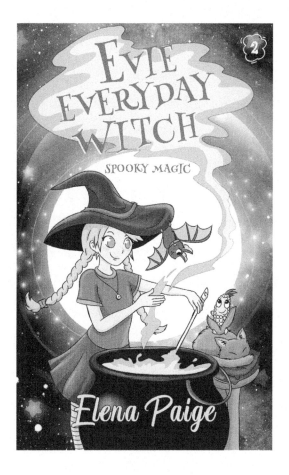

Visit
www.ElenaPaige.com

ABOUT THE AUTHOR

ELENA PAIGE loves creating stories which inspire and transform young readers. She writes from the heart and especially loves weaving magic into her books.

Her greatest value in life is creativity - nurturing it, enhancing it and using it. She loves inspiring children to believe in themselves and accept their own way of creating, even if it's outside the box. The most amazing creatives on the planet, rarely fitted in!

As a child, she thought magic was real and used to try convincing her teddy to come to life. Tired of waiting she adopted a Moodle dog, Lucky, that rarely leaves her side.

Find her at www.ElenaPaige.com

Made in the USA
Monee, IL
02 August 2020

37437461R10100